ABOUT THE AUTHOR

A former senior editor of *Fortune* magazine in New York City, Harold Burton Meyers was born August 2, 1924, in Arizona. He grew up on Indian reservations in the Southwest and is a graduate of the University of Colorado. He and his wife, Jean, live in Williamsburg, Virginia. They have four sons and three grandchildren.

ABOUT THE AWARD

The *National Novella Award* is an annual award of $2,500 plus publication for the best novella-length work of fiction. Cosponsored by the Arts and Humanities Council of Tulsa (publisher of *Nimrod* literary magazine) and Council Oak Books, the *National Novella Award* was established in recognition of the novella's increasing popularity and importance in the national culture.

For more information about the *National Novella Award* competition, write to the Arts and Humanities Council of Tulsa, Inc. at 2210 S. Main, Tulsa, OK 74114.

GERONIMO'S PONIES

GERONIMO'S PONIES

HAROLD BURTON MEYERS

NATIONAL NOVELLA AWARD

Council Oak Books, Tulsa, Oklahoma

Council Oak Books,
Tulsa, Oklahoma 74120

First Edition

Printed in the United States of America

LC 063117

ISBN 0-933031-18-1 (paper)

Cover design by Charles Swallow

For J.A.M. and all that
followed, with love.

1

We finished supper and sat on the front steps in the cool shade, watching shadows stretch over the patch of grass my father was trying against all odds to grow in the adobe soil. A Ford V-8 station wagon trailed dust past the trading post and turned down the hill toward the school. We didn't often see a strange car at Klinchee. We were far from any main road.

"Now who's this, do you suppose?" Pa said as the station wagon rattled over the cattle guard.

"It looks like Uncle Eph's old crate," I said. Uncle Eph was my mother's brother, one of many but always her favorite. He had come to visit several times before she fell sick, something none of her other brothers had done, and he was the only one she had corresponded with, even at Christmas.

"I think you're right."

"He's got somebody with him."

"Maybe he brought Muffie, though it doesn't seem likely. Funny he didn't let us know he was coming."

Muffie was Uncle Eph's wife, a big square-faced woman who wore loose dresses that fell straight from her shoulders to her ankles. She had taken up religion late in life, along about the time Uncle Eph got out of the oil business, and she had turned batty. When we took my mother home to Texas to bury her, all Aunt Muffie wanted to talk about was tablecloths. She kept trying to pin Pa and me down as to how many tablecloths my mother had owned and whether they were for family, company, or show. It was not something either of us had given thought to.

Uncle Eph unfolded out of the car like a carpenter's rule. He was a big man, taller than my father and fifty pounds heavier. Uncle Eph had the hands of a wrestler, which he had been in his young days, when he had joined a traveling carnival and taken on all comers without ever, he said, having been thrown. He dressed like a movie rancher, Tom Mix or Buck Jones, in high-heeled boots, tight twill pants, a two-tone shirt pulled taut over the belly, and a white ten-gallon hat.

My mother used to tease him about his costume, pointing out that their father, my grandfather, had been an actual rancher and mostly wore bib overalls and common work shoes, with a straw hat to keep off the sun. Uncle Eph said that kind of garb might have been all right for his daddy, but in these modern times a man had to dress his part to get ahead, had to announce by the way he dressed what manner of man he was and what in general his line of work might be. And who knows, he added, maybe if the old man had dressed for what he was — a landowner, a gentleman, an officer and hero of the Confederate Army — instead of like just another sodbuster, he might not have lost the ranch way back then and he, Uncle Eph, might have had a stake to work with instead of having to scratch every which way for every last dollar that ever came his way.

I ran down to the car. Uncle Eph picked me up and swung me around.

"Well, Davey," he said, "you just won't stop growing, will you? I can't hardly lift you no more. Keep shooting up like you are and before long you'll have just as much trouble as me fitting into a itty-bitty car like this. I been sitting all scooched up for so long I wasn't sure my joints was still working."

A short fat man came around from the passenger side. He was dressed like my grandfather in striped bib overalls, a blue work shirt with sweat circles under the arms, and dirt-crusted work shoes. The floppy brim of a big straw hat shadowed his face.

"Will," Uncle Eph said, "I want you to shake hands with Mr. Smart, best damned judge of horseflesh you'll ever hope to meet. Mr. Smart's from Oklahoma."

"How do," Mr. Smart said. He shook hands with me too. His hand looked and felt like a lump of biscuit dough ready to be rolled out.

"I suppose you brought Mr. Smart with you because of the horse auction I mentioned in my letter," Pa said as we hauled suitcases up the walk to the house.

"Damned tootin'," Uncle Eph said. "What you said about them horses just set my brain afire. I got hold of Mr. Smart fast as could be and jumped in the car. We drove straight through, not to waste a minute. Surprised you didn't see it yourself."

"See what?" I asked.

"Why, opportunity, boy, opportunity."

About a week earlier, my father had written to thank Uncle Eph for a snapshot he sent of the stone on my mother's grave, which he'd bought with money Pa gave him after the funeral. The photograph was blurred and had been taken between the legs of a lot of people standing around the grave. We couldn't read the words on the stone, but we were glad to know her burial place was properly marked. In his letter, Pa told Uncle Eph, mostly just to fill out the page, that Washington had ordered a reduction in the number of sheep and horses on the Navajo Indian Reservation, hoping to do something about the overgrazing that was turning the reservation into a wasteland. With nothing to hold the soil, wind devils now whirled where grass once grew as high as a horse's belly. Most of the excess sheep were already gone, and thousands of horses were to be rounded up and sold at a series of auctions, starting in the part of the reservation that Pa was in charge of.

At the time he wrote, Pa thought of the horse auction only as an interesting but harmless bit of news. He said later that he had failed to take into full account who was going to read the letter. Uncle Eph saw opportunity everywhere, and sometimes managed to grasp it. He had once made a million dollars speculating in land and built the biggest house Wichita Falls had seen up to that time. But Uncle Eph didn't know when to stop. He put everything he'd made or could borrow into buying more land just as the boom ended, wiping out both the million dollars and the house.

Something similar happened when he turned to wildcatting. He brought in a gusher about a day ahead of bankruptcy and started building a still bigger house in Wichita Falls — one so big he claimed you couldn't holler from one end of it to the other without a megaphone. When Standard Oil offered to buy his leases for a sum in the millions, Uncle Eph declared that he wasn't a man to deal with thieves. He was going to develop his oil field on his own and keep the profits himself instead of letting them flow into Rockefeller britches. Unfortunately, about the time he and Aunt Muffie moved into their new house, Uncle Eph's second well came in dry. So did the third. He went back to Standard Oil, but before he could strike a deal his first well went dry too. Pa said poor Eph's promising new oil field petered out quicker'n a mule could snatch a mouthful of hay, leaving him with nothing but three dry holes and a pocketful of debt. He and Aunt Muffie got to live in the new house only a short time. By the time his creditors were through with him, he wouldn't have been able to keep food on his table if my parents hadn't sent him a few dollars every month.

2

Around the kitchen table, over a supper of scrambled eggs and bacon, Uncle Eph spelled out for us the opportunity he had spotted. Mr. Smart dropped in a "yep" or a "just the way it were" now and again without, however, adding much content to the flow of conversation.

What Uncle Eph professed to see in the Indian ponies was nothing less than a chance to bring back prosperity, not just to himself but to all Texas. Those ponies would remind Texans that they were descendants of pioneers who tamed the West on horseback. The consequent resurgence of pride would do what Franklin Roosevelt and his New Deal had been unable to do, even well into a second term: Restore confidence and make the economy hum. Things would open up once Texans began thinking free and big again like their granddaddies, Uncle Eph said, instead of dragging around as though the overdue bills and mortgages they carried on their backs were made of solid lead. Men would go back to work. They'd have dollars in their pockets and smiles on their faces.

Women would sing and children frolic. The Dust Bowl would be stopped in its tracks. And all because of those little old Indian ponies my father had told him about.

Pa poured himself a cup of coffee. "Eph, you mind running through that again, a little slower? I bounced off your train of thought along about Lubbock and haven't caught up yet. How in hell is a bunch of broken-down horses going to do all that? Or any of it?"

"Will, just think on it a minute," Uncle Eph said. "What made Texas great? The horse. We all grew up on horseback, Will, me and you too. We was thinking big, doing big things, living well, making big money, getting rich. It was when we give up our horses that everything began to get all pinched-like. Little old houses with leaky roofs and cardboard in the windows in place of glass. Little old cars breaking down before they was even paid for. Little old tractors stinking up the countryside, and them breaking down too. No wonder people got to feeling hard up and lost their dreams. They just quit, was what they done — just hunkered down and let them eastern bankers and Rockefellers roll over 'em without no effort to fight back. Will, take my word for it. You just give a Texan a horse again and — "

"Eph," Pa said, "I know you and Mary were born on that ranch, but seems to me your daddy lost the place years before a car or tractor came onto it. As for me, my poor father didn't have a single horse, just a couple of mean old mules. I grew up following the wrong end of a mule down one furrow and then the next, hoping for not much more from the critter than to keep out of the way of its teeth and heels. So tell me how in God's name do you expect a bunch of Indian ponies — "

"You're not seeing it, Will, you're just not seeing it."

Mr. Smart, still wearing his straw hat as he shoveled eggs into his face, nodded his head vigorously. "Yep," he said. "Yep. Just the way it were."

It wasn't clear to me whose version of Texas's past and probable future Mr. Smart had endorsed, but Uncle Eph backed away from the big picture and began to sketch in details, speaking slowly as though to mental defectives, doggedly trying to make my father and me understand exactly what he had in mind. His plan was to buy those Indian ponies, or at least the better ones among them, feed them up and ship them down to Texas, where he predicted he would find a vast market for them as saddle horses for children. He was going to start with Fort Worth, it being a place that had some money and still thought of itself as a cow town. As soon as Uncle Eph ran a few ads in the papers, every little cowboy and cowgirl in Fort Worth — hell, in Texas — would be clamoring for an Indian pony of his or her own.

And the parents? Well, said Uncle Eph, he knew Texas parents about as well as anybody could, being one himself, though his and Muffie's kids were all grown and gone by now. Take his word for it, Uncle Eph said, or ask Muffie, whichever we wanted, but Texas parents would leap at the chance to restore their children to honest-to-God Texashood by putting them on horseback.

"Will," he said, "all you got to do is remind them folks that despite all their troubles they are by God Texans and it's time they get off their knees and start acting like it. You do that and the lines of people wanting to plunk down their money for these here Indian ponies is going to stretch from Fort Worth to Dallas."

Before Uncle Eph had shoveled down the last of his eggs, his pony fever had flared to such heights that he began worrying about inadequate supplies. He sounded my father out about the chances of more horse sales being held after this first round of auctions was over. Was there any way, he wondered, for him and Mr. Smart to get in ahead of the crowd with a bid for ponies to be offered at those future sales no one but Uncle Eph had started to think about yet? Pa said he doubted it. In any case, he said, if Uncle Eph came up with a way to collude with other problematical bidders at those as yet unscheduled and unplanned auctions, he certainly didn't want to hear about it.

Next Uncle Eph pondered the possibility of hooking up with a harness maker. Every one of those ponies was going to require furnishings. Uncle Eph couldn't see why, as the benefactor who first spotted the new need for ponies and started Texas back on the road to prosperity, he shouldn't get a little something out of the saddle and bridle business that was bound to spring up in his wake all across the state.

About the time I would normally have been heading for bed, Uncle Eph offered to cut my father in on the deal. The amounts mentioned floated through the room like so many balloons, starting at five thousand dollars but rapidly deflating to five hundred dollars or even, because of Pa's special brother-in-lawly status, as little as two hundred and fifty dollars. My father said he was honored, he surely was, to receive such an offer, but his further status as a government official with at least a peripheral responsibility for the success of auctions to be held in the district of which he was the supervisor would unfortunately preclude his joining Uncle Eph in the venture, even if he'd had the money to do so, which he didn't.

He also expressed a few doubts about the economics of the venture, putting his objections gently so as not to offend Uncle Eph. He pointed out that the ponies would be mostly wild and unbroken, of unknown age and dubious physical condition. To the extent possible, the Indians would be allowed to designate which horses should be sold, and it was not in human nature for them to retain old or decrepit animals while sending young and vigorous mounts to market.

Once purchased, the horses would have to be fed and watered and driven long distances to the railroad for shipment to Texas. Uncle Eph would have to recruit and pay a large crew of Navajo cowboys, who would themselves have to be fed and watered at his expense. Stock cars would be needed for the trip to Texas, and my father's understanding was that they would have to be ordered well in advance. Swift and Armour, which wanted the horses primarily for hides and other by-products, already had cars waiting on a Santa Fe siding down near Chambers. And what about feed and water on the trip to Texas, which might take several days, perhaps even a week or more? Finally, Pa asked, wouldn't somebody have to break those ponies to the saddle somewhere along the line? Surely Eph was not thinking of loosing wild broncos on the innocent children of Texas?

Uncle Eph took all this in stride. He regarded the difficulties my father pointed out as mere pebbles in the path of progress. None should be an insuperable obstacle to a man of spirit, certainly not to a true Texan, born and bred. Now and again, however, he pulled a dog-eared notebook out of his hip pocket and jotted down reminders to himself.

"Swift and Armour," he said, making a note. "Cudahy not here?"

"Oh, Cudahy's in it too," Pa said.

"Good," said Uncle Eph. "The more the merrier. I'll get together with them boys and see if we can't work it out so Mr. Smart and me take on the good stock and let them have the rest for their rendering plants. No reason we should get in each other's way, driving up prices."

"Eph, don't tell me about it. That's all I ask. Just don't tell me about it."

"Yep," Mr. Smart said. "That's the way it were."

Having Uncle Eph visit made me think about my mother even more than usual when I went to bed that night. I remembered how she had looked at me sometimes, deep in thoughts I could not fathom, her face still, her eyes on me but seeing something or someone else, beyond touch. It bothered me that she had died before I was old enough to understand what or who it was she saw when she looked at me like that.

3

My father had been holding meetings for months to explain to the Indians why stock reduction was necessary and how the plan would work. The final meeting was held soon after Uncle Eph's arrival, at Hosteen Tse's place at the base of Big Mesa, near Greasewood Wash. Hosteen Tse was a great Navajo medicine man and tribal leader who had attended all the earlier stock-reduction meetings. He was very old and as a child had gone on the Long Walk to Fort Sumner, New Mexico, which the Navajos called Hwalte. That is where the Navajos were sent into exile after Colonel Kit Carson and his troops rounded them up in 1863. Thousands of Navajos died at Hwalte before General William Tecumseh Sherman, the Union general who had marched through Georgia, arrived to negotiate a treaty in 1868.

As a medicine man, Hosteen Tse was not only priest, physician, and politician, but tribal historian and archivist as well. He knew not just the ancient chants and rituals, but all there was to know of importance to his family and tribe. Stored in his old brain was everything from clan relationships to all the details of every treaty or agreement signed with Washington since Sherman met with Barboncito and other Navajo chiefs at Hwalte.

Usually Pa wore khaki wash pants, a dress shirt buttoned to the throat, and no tie. Hot as it was, however, for this last meeting before the first horse auction he put on his good blue suit and a tie, along with a low-crowned grey Stetson he said was just a five-gallon size. I polished his good black shoes, which were made of kangaroo hide and came from the Monkey Ward catalog. He wore them only on the most special occasions.

We left for Big Mesa early in the morning because there was no proper road, only a wagon trail, leading to Hosteen Tse's hogans, and the going was slow. Pa drove his official car, a green Ford pickup truck with blue and white U.S. Indian Service license plates. Hosteen Begay, a Navajo assistant at Klinchee who was the official interpreter, rode with him. I went with Uncle Eph and Mr. Smart in the station wagon.

We got to Big Mesa a little before noon. Hosteen Tse had a large family encompassing several generations. A dozen or so log and mud hogans were scattered along the slope of Big Mesa's rocky base, along with open-sided summer shelters roofed with sagebrush and dried tumbleweeds. A little way off, half hidden, stood three small sweat houses, which served both practical and ceremonial purposes. Every so often, winter or summer, Hosteen Tse and his family heated the sweat houses with hot stones and crawled inside one or two at a time for as long as they could stand the heat. Then they piled out to cleanse themselves with sand and their own sweat, while chanting sacred songs of purification.

Ordinarily, few people would have been at Big Mesa because most Navajos had moved their flocks up into the Chuska Mountains for summer grazing. Word of the meeting had traveled over the reservation like drifting tumbleweeds, however, and for days Indians had been converging on Big Mesa. Wagons were drawn up all around the hogans when we arrived. Each visiting family had its own campfire, with a blackened tin can of coffee sitting in the hot coals. Most of the wagon teams were in a brush corral set up for the occasion, but a bunch of saddle horses dozed in the hot sun with heads drooping, reins looped over their necks or trailing in the dust. Women sat on the ground in the sparse shade of the wagons and shelters, spinning wool and tending the children who played around them. No men were in sight.

We sat for a few minutes, sweating in the hot vehicles. Then Pa got out and brushed dust off his suit coat. He and Hosteen Begay leaned against the pickup's front fenders, waiting for the men to appear. Uncle Eph, Mr. Smart and I stayed back out of the way, standing in a thin slice of midday shade beside a big boulder.

Uncle Eph worried about the size of the gathering.

"These folks look like trouble to me," he said. "Where you reckon the bucks is?"

"The old men are in the big hogan," I said, "and the rest are just staying out of sight until Hosteen Tse decides it's time to start." I had been to a lot of these meetings by then.

After a while young Indian men began drifting out from behind the hogans. They stood in a silent semicircle twenty feet or so from the pickup, legs astraddle and hands in the back pockets of their Levis. Ten-gallon hats topped angry faces, and spurs jangled as the men scraped boot toes in the dust. More men came out from inside the hogans until there were thirty or so.

Finally the elders emerged. They had come from all over the reservation, not just Pa's district, for this meeting. Hosteen Tse was the last to appear. He was hatless. His white hair was drawn back from his wrinkled old face and held in place by a dark blue bandanna, neatly rolled and wrapped around his head. He wore loose white trousers like pajama bottoms and a blue velveteen blouse cinched at the waist with a silver belt. On a chain around his neck hung a medal he had received when he and other Navajo leaders went to Washington decades earlier to meet with President McKinley. Over the years the medal had turned green.

My father did not usually smoke, but he passed around cigarettes. Each of the men took one and lit up, my father too. They smoked in silence, no one looking at anyone else. To stare directly at another person was considered rude, an act of disrespect and hostility.

As the senior Navajo present, it was up to Hosteen Tse to signal the start of the meeting. After the last cigarette was ground out underfoot, he greeted my father, calling him Mr. Tall Man American. "Yahehteh, Hosteen Nez Belihkahnah."

"Yahehteh, Hosteen Tse," Pa replied. He lifted his hat to the old man. His hair, turning gray since my mother died, was wet with sweat and plastered to his skull.

My father had been through his speech so many times that Hosteen Begay could have recited it by rote — Hosteen Tse too, most likely — but for form's sake Pa had to speak before Hosteen Begay could translate. The questions and protests that followed were familiar too, dealing mostly with charges of favoritism. For example, why were families at Klinchee being allowed to keep more horses than Big Mesa families? My father knew that was not true, but it would have been insulting for him to say so. "I do not believe that is the case," he said, "but I shall look into it and stop it if it is happening, because that would not be fair."

Hosteen Tse usually said nothing after his opening words. He listened carefully but made no comment. At this last meeting before the start of the auctions, however, he made a speech when everyone else was done talking. He spoke in short bursts. Between bursts, Hosteen Begay translated, keeping his eyes respectfully on the ground at the old man's feet.

"When I was a little child," said Hosteen Tse, "my people could fight no longer and Kit Carson took us to Hwalte and kept us there. It was a jail without bars where soldiers guarded us. Times were hard and we were poor. We had no sheep, no crops. We ran out of wood for our fires. Many people died in the cold. When they tried to go home soldiers caught them and marched them back to Hwalte, pointing guns at them but giving them no food. Then General Sherman came and promised to let us return to our homes if we promised to quit fighting and live in peace. This we agreed to do in return for sheep and schools and hospitals.

"We made promises and kept them. You made promises and did not keep them. Where are the schools for every thirty students? The teachers? The hospitals? The blacksmith shops, carpenter shops, the men who would teach us to farm? Many times have we gone to Washington to ask why you do not keep your promises. All you give us is more promises — and this."

He held up the corroded medal he wore around his neck, the medal given him by President McKinley. He waved it back and forth in front of his face.

He was silent for a long time before he went on. "We have done what we must do to live, and now you tell us we cannot keep our sheep and our horses. How are we to live when you take away our sheep and our horses? Are we to live on the promises you do not keep?"

He stopped again, waiting. My father had no answer. I had heard him say many times pretty much what Hosteen Tse had just said, but he could not say it here, not before these people for whom he was not just Will Parker, a man entitled to speak his own mind, but Hosteen Nez Belihkahnah, official representative of the U.S. Government.

Hosteen Tse looked him in the eye and spat in the dust at his feet.

That evening when we were home and talking over the day, Uncle Eph said, "Will, you hadn't ought to let that shifty-eyed old heathen spit at you like that."

"I swear, Eph," Pa said, "there's times I can't tell you from a fool."

Mr. Smart said, "Yep, that's the way it were."

4

We could see the dust rising miles off as Navajo cowboys drove horses to auction in bunches that grew into herds. By the day of the first sale, hundreds of horses milled in temporary corrals of brush and logs on the sagebrush flats near Klinchee. Indian families came from all over the reservation to watch the sale, and the government put on a feed. Mrs. Tsinnijinni, the school cook, fixed beans and salt pork in washtubs and boiled Arbuckle's coffee in milk cans, which Hosteen Begay and my father helped lift on and off the stove. I opened gallon tins of stewed tomatoes and peanut butter from the school warehouse. Navajo men took charge of roasting whole sheep over open fires they built in the school yard, while women made bread. They tossed the dough from hand to hand to lighten it with air and then dropped it into pans of boiling mutton fat. Soon there were washtubs full of fried bread for the noon feast.

The auctioneer had been brought in from Albuquerque. He put up a big tent near the corrals and rolled up the sides to let the air through. Then he backed a flatbed truck into the tent for a platform. Plank tables and benches were set up on the truck for the auctioneer and the government officials, my father among them, who were to oversee the sale.

Before the auction began, the cowboys sorted the horses into lots of ten, each lot in a separate, numbered pen. I tagged along after Uncle Eph and Mr. Smart as they circulated among the buyers from big slaughter houses who were examining the horses and deciding how high to bid on each lot. The buyers were mostly Texans like Uncle Eph, but between their cowboy boots and broad-brimmed hats they wore business suits with dress shirts and ties. They all knew one another and joked and laughed, falling silent as we came up. It was clear that they regarded Uncle Eph, fellow Texan or not, as a rank outsider, but he acted as though the buyers were as glad to meet him and Mr. Smart as he said he was to meet them.

Each time Uncle Eph introduced himself, he commented that he had never encountered a sorrier display of horseflesh. According to him, out of all the hundreds of horses in the pens, not more than a handful deserved to be called Indian ponies, suitable for young Texans to ride. The rest of the puny critters were good for nothing but dog food, and the buyers' companies were doing a real service by being willing to take the poor brutes off the Indians' hands. It was too bad, though, Uncle Eph said, that the prices everyone would have to pay were likely to be unjustly high. He and Mr. Smart would be compelled to bid on damned near every lot, seeking that one animal or two per lot they might be justified in taking to Texas as a child's mount. A pity.

The buyers stood around like Navajos, keeping their eyes on some distant point as Uncle Eph talked, and they spoke in monosyllables if at all. But more was going on than I caught on to, because after a while the other buyers joined Uncle Eph and Mr. Smart in approaching the auction officials to seek a change of procedure. Uncle Eph was the spokesman for the group, proposing that the better horses be pulled out and auctioned in separate lots. This would not lower the value of the lots destined for the dogfood factories and rendering plants, he argued, but would mean higher prices — deservedly higher, Uncle Eph said — for the more valuable animals.

Pa removed himself from the discussion between the buyers and the officials. He took me over to the trading post to buy a bottle of soda pop. "Damn these horses," he said. "I wish I'd never told Eph about them. He's going to have us all in jail."

By the time we got back to the tent, cowboys were sorting out the ponies pointed out by Mr. Smart and forming them into new lots. The cowboys weren't too careful in their work and some shaky old nags got included with the good horses. Nevertheless, Uncle Eph was pleased with the way things had turned out in his dealings with the other buyers. "Most men is tight as Dick's hatband," he said, "but they'll listen to reason when it don't cost them nothing."

After the noontime feasting was over, the auction started and moved along rapidly. Each lot took only a few minutes to dispose of and each drew about the same price, a dollar or two per animal. The buyers took turns making the winning bid on each lot. It went alphabetically: Armour, Cudahy, Swift, Wilson, with other buyers fitting in according to the initial letter of their companies' names. The auctioneer joked about this happenstance, as he called it, but my father and the other government officials were not amused. They called a halt to the sale while my father warned the buyers that any question of collusion would be referred to the proper authorities. The pattern became a little more intricate when the sale resumed, but the bidding continued perfunctory and the corporate buyers still took turns being the successful bidder.

The lots made up of better horses were sold last. Up to then, Uncle Eph and Mr. Smart had been standing over at one side of the tent with me. They watched but did not say anything. Now they moved down front.

The auctioneer started the bidding at about double the price the other lots had gone for. Uncle Eph lifted his hat and resettled it on his head, signaling a bid. Then he gazed up at the top of the tent as though he'd done his all and had no further interest in the proceedings.

The auctioneer went through his spiel asking for a higher bid and was calling out, "Going, going . . ," when he got the new bid he had asked for. It came from the Swift man. Uncle Eph looked pained, but he lifted his hat again. Then more bidders got into it. Uncle Eph ultimately bought that lot and the others he wanted, but he wound up paying many times what he had counted on.

He felt he had been double-crossed by the other buyers but blamed himself for being taken in. "I shoulda knowed better than trust a company man," he said. "One thing I learned from Standard Oil is that the only snake lower'n a corporation is the son of a sea cook who'll work for one."

5

I hoped to get a pony for myself from among the horses Uncle Eph bought. He argued on my behalf, even offering to give me one free.

"Will, you just ain't raising this boy like a Texas boy ought to be raised," Uncle Eph said. "I aim to let him have his pick of the litter."

Pa put his foot down and would not budge. He pointed out that anytime he or I wanted to ride we had only to go up to the trading post and hire a horse, already saddled and bridled, for maybe a quarter a day from one of the Navajo men who spent their time squatting in the shade while their mounts trailed reins in the dust. If we bought a horse, we'd have not only its care and feeding to deal with, but also the problem of a place to keep it. There was no corral or stable at Klinchee Day School, and no provision in the government's planning for any. And with him having to drive from school to school most days, making sure everything in his district was running smoothly, and with me generally going along, doing my lessons there beside him in the front of his pickup truck, we had no time to spare for a horse.

To make up for denying me a pony, Pa agreed to let me go to Texas for two weeks while Uncle Eph sold the Indian horses. The night before we were to leave Pa came to my room to tuck me in. He gave me a leather billfold — my first real wallet. There were three new ten-dollar bills in it.

"I'm going to miss you, son," he said, hugging me.

"Yessir," I said. Excited as I was about getting to go with Uncle Eph, I felt a little like crying.

"The money in that billfold ought to be more than enough to live on and buy your bus ticket home."

"Yessir."

"I've got a new belt for you, too," he said, "and there's something special about this belt. It's got a secret compartment in it, and I've hidden two more ten-dollar bills in there for you."

He showed me the secret compartment and the ten-dollar bills. I had never dreamed of having so much money.

"Now, Davey, this is important."

"Yessir."

"I don't want you to tell anybody — not anybody at all — about this hidden money."

"Yessir."

"And I mean Uncle Eph too."

"Sir?"

"I mean you are not to tell Uncle Eph about the twenty dollars in your belt. If things get tight and all the money in the billfold is gone and Uncle Eph says, 'Davey, don't you have any more money?' I want you to say, 'Nosir.'"

I could hardly believe my ears.

He read my mind. "I'm telling you to lie if you have to, Davey. I don't like doing it but it's necessary, take my word for it. You can give Uncle Eph every other cent you've got, but I want you to keep this money so if things don't go the way you think they should you can walk away and get to a bus station and buy a ticket home. The one thing you are not to do is give this money to Uncle Eph or even admit you've got it. I want you to promise me that."

I promised.

"And if things get beyond you, ask Mr. Smart for help. He strikes me as a sensible man, despite getting mixed up in this bird-brained scheme of Eph's."

6

We all went to the railroad to help load the horses into stock cars. My father drove our old Dodge, riding alone. I settled down in the back seat of the Ford station wagon, ready for the trip to Texas, with Uncle Eph driving and Mr. Smart dozing beside him. From Klinchee to Chambers, where the loading pens were, the carcasses of dead horses littered the desert, their bloated bellies ripped open by coyotes and buzzards. Some of the animals that had died on the long run to the railroad were Uncle Eph's. He damned the government for requiring the herds to be moved off the reservation too fast, without sufficient time for rest and grazing.

"A horse has got to graze," Uncle Eph said. "Grazing to a horse is like me putting my feet up at the end of a hard day and maybe taking a little nip."

"That's the way it were," Mr. Sharp said.

The stock cars were supposed to be waiting on the siding so there'd be plenty of time to load before the midnight freight stopped to pick them up, but when we got to Chambers we found nothing on the siding but bare track. It was almost dark before a coal-burning switch engine arrived, pushing the empty cars ahead of it.

As soon as the engine chugged up, whistling and spilling steam, the horses spooked. They began milling in the log corrals and kept milling. By the time it was full dark, Uncle Eph's Navajo cowboys had not been able to prod a single horse into the loading chute and over the plank bridge into a stock car. To cut the darkness enough for the cowboys to see a little bit of what they were doing, Uncle Eph and Pa aimed their car lights at the chute through the cracks between the logs. We could see the horses circling in the corrals, wild-eyed, hooves pounding, as alternate stripes of light and dark played over their backs. They looked like rampaging zebras. The cowboys rushed them, pushed them, roped them, whipped them. Nothing worked. Every time a pony neared the open chute it whirled away, refusing to go in.

Uncle Eph was getting desperate.

"Listen, fellas," he said, "that train's gonna be here before you know it and these horses has got to go out on it. It's time you quit fooling around and got down to business."

"No savvy," the cowboys said.

"Where the hell's the foreman?"

One of the cowboys grunted and stuck out his lower lip in a quick gesture, pointing toward the railroad cars.

"He says the foreman's over there," I told Uncle Eph.

We found the foreman asleep on the track under one of the cars. Uncle Eph pulled him out and shook him.

"Drunk," he said. "I should've knowed."

He hauled the man off the tracks and stretched him out in the ditch to sleep it off. We went back to the loading chute.

"I don't know how in hell we're going to get them damned horses to climb in them cars," Uncle Eph said. He took off his hat and wiped his sweaty forehead with his arm.

"Blindfold 'em," Mr. Smart said.

Uncle Eph looked at him like he was seeing Jesus on the water.

"Of course," Uncle Eph said. "Mr. Smart, you done lived up to your name again."

He ran to the station wagon and came back with a half-dozen shirts. But when he tried to explain what he wanted, the cowboys stared at him blankly. He tried it again, louder this time.

"It doesn't do any good to turn up the volume," Pa said. "Let me try." He spoke a few words in Navajo, pantomiming as he went.

The cowboys started wrapping shirts around horses' heads. One after another, the blindfolded and suddenly docile creatures marched into the chutes.

"Lucky thing you know the lingo," Uncle Eph said, "or we'd been here all night and missed the damned train."

"The men knew what you wanted done," Pa said. "They just didn't care for the way you told them to do it."

The last of the ponies entered the cars as the freight whistled in the distance. Uncle Eph paid off the cowboys and we stood by the tracks to watch the train head for Texas.

"Let's get going," Uncle Eph said. "I want to make Tucumcari by morning."

I hopped in the back end of the station wagon.

"Remember your promise, Davey," Pa yelled after me.

"I will," I yelled back. I waved out the back window as long as I could see him standing in the lights of the Dodge.

"What's the promise?" Uncle Eph asked, looking over his shoulder at me. "Be a good boy and all that?"

"Yessir," I said.

"I ain't worried about that," Uncle Eph said. "You just do what I tell you and do it when I tell you to and we'll get along just fine."

"Yessir."

"And the first thing I'm telling you to do is stretch out back there and go to sleep."

It seemed like only a few minutes before the sun was in my eyes. The car was stopped and when I sat up there was no one in the front seat. For a moment I was scared. I looked around and saw Uncle Eph coming out the door of a roadside café picking his teeth and carrying a bottle of NeHi Orange soda pop and a paper sack. Mr. Smart was heading into a Chick Sales behind the café.

"You all right, boy?" Uncle Eph said. He looked tired. His eyes were bloodshot and he hadn't shaved.

"Yessir," I said.

After Mr. Smart came out, I went to use the Chick Sales. It was a three-holer with no toilet paper, just a torn up Wards catalog, and the smell was awful. I got out as fast as I could. I looked around for a place to wash my hands, but there wasn't any.

Uncle Eph was already at the wheel with Mr. Smart beside him.

"Load up, boy," Uncle Eph said. "We gotta move out."

I got in the back seat and he handed me the NeHi Orange and the paper sack he had brought out of the café. There was a greasy hamburger in the sack, along with a piece of crumbly chocolate cake wrapped in a napkin.

"Where are we?" I asked, chewing on the hamburger.

Uncle Eph was driving fast. The car's shadow raced alongside us, climbing up and down the ditch bank, whipping over sagebrush. The road curved and we drove straight into the sun. It was still only a little above the horizon.

"Past Tucumcari," Uncle Eph said, shielding his eyes with his hand, "heading to Amarillo. We're going to have our first sale there, the Lord willing, and we gotta move fast to get things organized. Got to get the sales yard lined up, an auctioneer, ads in the paper, posters out, all that kind of thing."

"I thought you said Fort Worth was first."

"Feeding them animals is expensive and moving them is more so," Uncle Eph said, "and Amarillo is a hell of a lot closer than Fort Worth."

Mr. Smart had his head thrown back and his face covered by his hat. I thought he was asleep.

"That's the way it were," he said.

7

Uncle Eph pulled into a tourist court on the edge of Amarillo. "Turth's Cabins," the sign said, "$1 a night."

Uncle Eph went inside. Through the window I saw him hug a big woman with bright red hair. She looked out at the car and waved. I waved back and after a moment Uncle Eph came out with a key in his hand.

"Old friends," Uncle Eph said.

We drove down a dusty lane between two rows of unpainted cabins. In front of No. 12 Uncle Eph stopped. Inside were two double beds and a cot, along with a coal range, an empty scuttle, and a washstand with a bucket and tin basin. Over the washstand hung a calendar put out by a local undertaker. The picture on the calendar was called "The End of the Trail." It showed an Indian warrior slumping on the back of a horse that looked near as dead as some of those we'd seen on the drive to the railroad. There were no sheets or blankets on the beds. The mattresses were stained and dirty. So was the cot.

"Toilet's across the way," Uncle Eph said. He took off his boots and stretched out on one of the beds. "Boy, while I take me a nap you go out and find a store. Buy some coffee, bread, and sliced ham. Mustard. Cheese if they got it. Milk if you want it."

I waited for him to give me some money. He closed his eyes. I looked at Mr. Smart, but he was sitting on the edge of the other bed taking off his shoes.

"What you waiting for, boy?" Uncle Eph said.

I went out and wandered around for a while. We were in a part of town without sidewalks. Mostly there were used car lots, hamburger joints, and service stations, but one of the service stations turned out to be a general store too. I got the stuff Uncle Eph asked for, along with a couple of bottles of NeHi Orange instead of milk. I spent more than a dollar. When I got back to the cabin, Uncle Eph and Mr. Smart were asleep.

Waiting for them to wake up, I sat on the front steps. It was hot, with no air moving. I could hear the whine of tires from cars traveling fast on the highway past Turth's Cabins. I was feeling pretty lonely. My trip with Uncle Eph was not turning out as I had thought it would, and he seemed like a different person when my father wasn't around.

I did not care for Turth's Cabins. I was not used to sleeping on dirty mattresses without sheets, and the people I saw coming in and out of the other cabins did not look like people I wanted to know. The men were unshaven and shaggy haired. They wore dirty overalls and ripped shirts. Their teeth were yellow and broken, or missing. The women were of two kinds — some with uncombed hair and no makeup, slumping around in dirty house dresses, and others with marcelled hair and layers of rouge on their faces, strutting by in tight skirts and high heels.

I saw only one person near my age, a girl dressed in bright pink pajamas, not the kind you sleep in but the billowy sort women used to wear to look like movie stars. She shot one glance at me as she walked past but did not say anything. She was dark and had glossy black hair flowing down her back to her waist. She looked like she might have Indian blood. I thought she was as pretty a girl as I'd ever seen.

Nobody else paid attention to me sitting there on the stoop of No. 12. I went in and got one of the bottles of NeHi Orange.

Uncle Eph sat up. He rubbed the back of his hand over his mouth.

"What time is it, boy?"

"I don't know, sir."

"Is it late?"

"Nosir."

He swung his feet onto the floor and pulled on his boots. He dug through a suitcase, brought out a set of fresh clothes, and went over to the washroom. When he came back he was shaved and his hair was wet and combed. He was dressed in tan pants and a fancy three-toned green shirt.

"Come shine me up, boy," he said. He sat on the edge of the bed and handed me a can of polish and a cloth.

I got down in front of him and polished his boots. When I finished he tousled my hair.

"Now let's eat, boy."

While Mr. Smart continued to snore on his bed, Uncle Eph slapped ham and cheese between a couple of slices of bread coated with mustard. He opened the other bottle of NeHi Orange and started eating.

I made myself a sandwich too. I was still eating when Uncle Eph finished.

"Well, let's go," he said. He stood up and smoothed his pants over his thighs.

"What about Mr. Smart?"

"Don't you worry about Mr. Smart. Ain't much for him to do till the horses get here."

We got in the station wagon and drove to a print shop. Uncle Eph left me in the car while he went in. When he came back he was chuckling.

"If you was a few years older, boy, I could tell you a hell of a funny story," he said.

From the print shop we went to an auctioneer's office and then to the Potter County Fairgrounds, where Uncle Eph walked around with the auctioneer to look over the sales yard. Most of the time I was sitting in the car, not knowing what Uncle Eph was up to and feeling like I was getting fried through in the heat. By the end of the afternoon, though, Uncle Eph was more like his old self.

"Boy," he said, "you're going to see you a real Texas-size blowout — big stripey tents, refreshment stands, even got us a band and a parade all set up. Now all we got left to do is get them ads in the paper and posters up."

We drove back to the print shop and he sent me inside to pick up the posters. There were a lot of them, bearing big red letters on yellow cardboard:

Put Texas Back
On Horseback

BIG SALE!!
A Rare Chance to Own
GERONIMO'S PONIES!!!
Tough *Spirited*
TAME!!
Place: ____________________
Time: ____________________
COME ONE COME ALL
Bring the family!
Refreshments!!!

The printer helped me carry the posters out to the station wagon and slide them into the back end.

"That'll be three bucks," the printer said.

Uncle Eph sat up behind the wheel and dug in his pocket.

"Damn," he said. "I must of left my billfold back to the cabin. Davey, you got any money on you?"

"Yessir," I said.

"You go ahead and pay him then."

"Yessir."

I gave the printer the money. He patted me on the head as he tucked the bills into a pocket of his inky apron.

"Uncle Eph," I said, "Geronimo wasn't a Navajo. He was an Apache."

"Hell, boy, you think I don't know that? But these folks here don't know it and wouldn't care if they did. When you say Geronimo they think Injun, mean Injun, and that's what gets their attention. These ain't ordinary, run-of-the-reservation, any old Indian's ponies, boy. These here is ponies they can brag on, Geronimo's ponies, and you keep that in mind."

We drove to the newspaper office and radio station, where Uncle Eph arranged to run ads on credit, and then we went back to Turth's Cabins. Mr. Smart was up and gone. Uncle Eph said he was down at the railroad. The Indian ponies were due in most any time. Uncle Eph got a big black crayon and filled in the time and place blanks on the posters. Then we drove around town nailing them on telephone poles at prominent corners and standing them in the windows of stores and service stations.

Uncle Eph knew just where to put the posters to get the most attention. "I know Amarillo like the back of my hand," he told me, and he did. Every place we went he knew someone.

Just before we quit and headed home to Turth's Cabins, he went into a store to drop off one last poster and came out with some beer and a chunk of ice. He seemed to have found his billfold, or maybe the storekeeper extended credit, because he didn't ask me to pay for the beer.

Back at the cabin he put the beer bottles in a bucket and packed it full of ice. He took off his boots and stretched out on the bed.

"Well, Davey," he said, sitting up to take a swig of beer, "we done a good day's work."

"Yessir."

"You fix you a ham sandwich for supper, if you want, or you can go out and buy you a hamburger if you'd rather. I got me a business meeting tonight and I don't expect I'll be back much afore morning. You know about business meetings, Davey?"

"Yessir." I didn't know for sure what he was telling me, but I guessed the answer he wanted.

He left, taking the bucket of ice and beer with him. I ate a ham sandwich and sat on the stoop, batting mosquitoes off my neck and arms.

The girl in pink pajamas came by. She started to walk past and then veered toward me.

"What's your name?" she asked. "I'm Clotie."

"Davey," I said.

"You want to fuck?"

I felt myself turning red. She was staring hard at me, and I looked away. I didn't know what to say. I knew whatever I said would be wrong.

"I'd let you for four bits."

"I guess not."

"Two bits?"

"No."

She shrugged. "I told him you wouldn't," she said. I thought she sounded relieved.

"Told who?"

"Your old man."

"Uncle Eph? He's not my father."

"That's not what he said."

"When did he say that?"

"Just now. He's got my ma for all night over in No. 7, and he told me to ask you could I sleep with you."

"Well, you can't," I said. "Not with me."

"I don't have no place to sleep then. He give me a dime to stay out of the way, you see."

"There's a cot. You could have that."

"All right."

It grew dark and the mosquitoes got bad. We went in. She brought out a pack of cards and we played a few hands of blackjack, but it wasn't much fun. We went to bed, her on the cot and me on Uncle Eph's mattress.

In a little while I heard her crying, so softly it was like breathing. I didn't know what to do. She kept on crying and finally I said, "What's wrong? Did I do something wrong?"

"I didn't want to say that to you," she said.

"That's all right," I said. "I didn't think you did."

"And I wouldn't done it if'n you'd said yes."

"I knew that," I said, though I couldn't help wondering if that was true and what it would have been like.

When I woke up the next morning, Uncle Eph was flat on his back beside me, one arm thrown across my chest. Mr. Smart snored noisily in the other bed. Clotie was gone.

My new billfold was gone too, with all the money in it.

Uncle Eph laughed. "You better go ask your little pink sweetheart about that," he said.

He took Mr. Smart and me downtown to a fancy hotel restaurant with tablecloths and bought breakfast. He paid with a new ten-dollar bill.

8

Uncle Eph outfitted me at J.C. Penney so I could ride in the parade before the sale. He bought me cowboy boots, a big white hat, and a red kerchief to wrap around my neck. When he asked if I had any money, I did like Pa told me and said no. Uncle Eph said that was all right, he'd pay for my clothes and Pa could reimburse him later. I was to ride one of the tame ponies Mr. Smart had found among the horses delivered by the Santa Fe. "About a dozen of them animals is saddle-broke enough," Mr. Smart said, "to be rode by timid girls and pregnant mammas."

Saturday was a hot day, up around a hundred before noon. Uncle Eph put me bareback on a skinny old bay with ribs that stuck out like barrel staves. He handed me one end of a rope that was looped around the necks of three other tame horses.

"Now all you got to do, boy, is stay on that horse," he said. "I want you to go riding along with a big grin on your face like there ain't nothing in this world you'd rather be doing than sitting on that there pony holding the rope to them other ponies, riding along after the band, having yourself a good time."

"Will the other horses be in the parade?" I asked. "The wild ones?"

"Don't worry about them," he said. "When we need 'em, Mr. Smart'll have 'em ready."

The band was late turning up. I'd been sitting on the horse in the hot sun so long that its sweat and mine had drenched my pants. I was sure everyone would think I'd wet myself.

The bandleader wanted to be paid before the parade. Uncle Eph argued a while before he discovered he'd left his wallet back at the cabin.

"Boy," he yelled, "you sure you don't have no money on you?"

"I'm sure, Uncle Eph," I said. My belt with the hidden ten-dollar bills felt like it was going to pinch me in two.

Uncle Eph threw his arm around the bandleader's shoulders and walked off with him a little way. When they came back, the bandleader had a couple of bills in his hand.

I rode through the streets of Amarillo with the band playing and majorettes twirling batons. Boys ran alongside handing out fliers about the big sale of Geronimo's ponies down at the fairgrounds. What with the posters and the newspaper and radio ads, a lot of people had turned out for the parade in spite of the heat.

I enjoyed the attention we drew, even while I worried whether the poor old pony I was on would keep going long enough to get me to the fairgrounds. Every once in a while the horse would stop and droop its head, like it was taking a quick snooze, and not start up again until I kicked it in the ribs a half-dozen times. On one corner I saw Clotie in her bright pink pajamas. I waved, but she pretended not to know me.

At the fairgrounds Uncle Eph put me in charge of the lemonade stand. He gave me a little sack of whole lemons and a big sack of lemon hulls, which he had found in the alley behind the hotel where we'd had breakfast downtown. He also gave me a sugar dispenser that had been on our table at the hotel, two big glass pitchers, and several tin cups. My instructions were simple — don't squeeze more than two lemons to a pitcher of water and go easy on the sugar. He said half a dozen lemon hulls in the bottom would be ample to give a rich look to the pitcher, not to mention a sharper flavor.

Uncle Eph opened the sale with a rousing speech about the importance of the horse in Texas's history and economy. It was about like the spiel he gave Pa and me when he first arrived at Klinchee to buy ponies, but he worked in some added licks about the character-building advantages of horse ownership for kids. The way Uncle Eph saw it, the care and feeding of a horse would teach boys and girls responsibility, keep them out of pool halls, and pretty much repair any parent-worrying defects of thought and behavior that the schools and churches weren't getting to. Heads nodded in agreement as he went along, and he got a big hand at the end.

I didn't see much of the day's proceedings after that, but every now and again I'd leave the lemonade stand in charge of Mr. Smart, put a grin on my face, and ride a pony into the auction ring, just to remind the folks what fun a kid could have on horseback. The cowboys drove the wild horses — spirited mounts, the auctioneer called them — into the ring one by one, riderless. Anyone who happened to be nearby and on foot ducked and dodged, trying to look unconcerned about flying hooves and snapping teeth.

By the end of the day most of the tame horses, but not the old bay I'd ridden in the parade, and a number of wild ones had been sold. Uncle Eph made a speech, congratulating the crowd and himself on the success of the auction and predicting an almost immediate return of prosperity and morality now that the horse was coming back to Texas. He invited everyone to stay on for a free band concert and then a barbecue over on the other side of the fairgrounds as soon as the sun went down. The band played "The Eyes of Texas."

Uncle Eph came by the lemonade stand and grabbed my cashbox.

"Let's go, boy," he said.

"What about the barbecue?"

"What barbecue?"

6

From Amarillo we drove through the Red River Valley to Owchita, but without the ponies, which were traveling on to Wichita Falls. Owchita was the little town where Uncle Eph lived, not far from the ranch he and my mother grew up on. On the way in we stopped by the graveyard where my mother was buried. She lay at the feet of her mother and father and beside a younger sister who had died in infancy. There was no stone on my mother's grave.

I asked Uncle Eph about it. He snapped his fingers.

"Them damned vandals," he said. "Ain't nothing sacred no more."

"You mean there was a stone there?"

"I sent you a picture of it, didn't I?"

"Yessir," I said. "I guess that's right."

We stayed only a few minutes at the cemetery and then Uncle Eph drove Mr. Smart and me out south of town to a locked gate on the dirt road leading to what had been my grandfather's spread. We leaned against the gate and looked out over an empty expanse, nothing to be seen but summer-browned grass and a couple of steers on the distant horizon. An Englishman owned all this land now, my grandfather's and that of a lot of other small ranchers and homesteaders. No one was allowed on the Englishman's land without permission.

"He was a great man, boy, don't you forget it," Uncle Eph said, taking off his hat and placing it against his chest. He was referring to my grandfather, of course, not the Englishman.

I was angry about the gravestone but didn't know what to do about it. I said, "Pa says when you come right down to it he was just a farmer, like Pa's daddy."

"Will Parker's a goddam liar," Uncle Eph said. "His old man was nothing but a dirt-poor nester with shit on his boots and cotton in his head, but your ma's daddy — my daddy too, your grandpa — he owned all this here land far as you can see. He was a rancher, a man of good family, a Confederate officer in the War Between the States, and a hero besides."

I didn't like him calling my father a liar. I said, "Ma said Grandpa wasn't really an officer. She said he was just a private who gave himself a peacetime promotion after he got out of the Army and married Grandma."

"Your ma didn't always speak of her daddy with the respect he deserved. He was a major in the cavalry of the Confederate States of America, boy, and you better remember that if you want me to have anything to do with you."

"That's the way it were, boy," Mr. Smart said.

At first I wondered what he knew about it, and then I realized he was warning me to drop the subject.

"Yessir," I said.

We went back through town by way of the square. In front of the courthouse stood a statue of a Confederate infantryman with a rifle almost as tall as he. My mother had told me about the statue. Her father wanted a mounted cavalryman, but the horse would have added too much to the cost, so the county commissioners sent off for a Zouave, buying it from a Yankee mail-order house in St. Joe that specialized in Confederate memorials. The soldier's trousers were just as baggy as she'd said they were.

I went over and looked closely at the statue. There were several small dents in the bronze.

"Are those from when Uncle Dunc shot at the bankrobbers?" I asked.

"What do you know about that, boy?" Uncle Eph seemed surprised that I had heard about Uncle Dunc.

"Ma said he was the town marshal but didn't have real good eyes and mistook the statue for a bankrobber."

"Your ma was a real little girl when Dunc got hisself killed," Uncle Eph said, "and I reckon that's why she didn't tell it just right. It was the robbers shot up the statue."

I didn't really believe him, preferring as I did my mother's account and trusting it more, but I listened as Uncle Eph went on.

"Dunc, he was behind the statue taking what cover he could, and it was the robbers out front of it shooting at him that put them pits in it. They was shooting like an army but didn't hit him but once, right through the eye. Over here's where they found him, not a bullet left in his gun. And out there in front was one of the robbers, so full of holes we had to wait six months for him to get well enough to hang."

My mother had told me about the robber being shot, not by Uncle Dunc but by a couple of cowhands who happened to be passing. She told me about the hanging too. The gallows was set up right in the middle of the town square and all the school children were marched over to stand in rows at one side, where they would have a clear sight of the wages of sin. She was only a first-grader, but as the sister of the murderer's victim she was given a place of honor in the front row, so close she could see sweat beading the young man's face as they blindfolded him and put the rope around his neck. The platform was built with open sides so that everyone would be able to watch the hanged man's death struggle. When the trap was sprung she turned her back and closed her eyes. The teacher scolded her there in front of everyone and made her look at the body jumping at the end of the rope. She was still sobbing and throwing up when Uncle Eph came to carry her home. Later he stopped her other brothers from teasing her for being so tenderhearted.

Uncle Eph took me inside the courthouse to see a dusty glass case of war memorabilia: bits of uniforms and a couple of medals, along with a sword which a printed card said had been carried at the Battle of Vicksburg by Maj. Amos Gower.

"See there?" Uncle Eph said. "A major, like I been telling you."

"Yessir," I said.

On the wall beside the case was a big photograph of Teddy Roosevelt the day he came through Owchita on his way to Indian Territory for hunting.

"That was a day," Uncle Eph said. "There's your grandpa, standing right next to the President on the courthouse steps, and see whose hand Teddy is shaking? Your ma's. He looked at her, Teddy Roosevelt did, and you know what he said? Bully, he said. That's what everybody who ever looked at Mary said, you got to keep that in mind. Wasn't just him. It was anybody — that little old girl was just so pretty and sassy, bully was about the least thing you could say."

I looked closely at the picture, one of the few I had ever seen of my mother as a child and the first I had seen of either of her parents. She had told me about shaking hands with Teddy Roosevelt as a girl, but hadn't mentioned having her picture taken with him. She was about my age in the photograph, perhaps a little older, and I thought she was beautiful as she smiled up at the President. Beside her my grandfather was a towering giant in bib overalls, looming over both her and the President. A big straw hat shaded my grandfather's face. All I could make out was a black beard with a white line that might have been teeth in the middle of it, which suggested he was smiling as Teddy Roosevelt shook his little daughter's hand. I was surprised. My mother had told me my grandfather fought the War to the last day of his life, and yet here he was, caught for all time, smiling at a Yankee President, a Republican at that.

From the courthouse we drove on to Uncle Eph's house. It was an unpainted cottage next door to a second-hand furniture store that Aunt Muffie ran, trying to make ends meet while Uncle Eph was off getting rich.

Aunt Muffie got out of a rocking chair on the porch of the store as we drove up.

"Praise the Lord!" she shouted.

She came out to the car. "You, boy," she said, "I been worrying about your immortal soul. Even wrote to Judge Rutherford — "

"Now, Muffie," Uncle Eph said, trying to grab her for a kiss.

She wrestled out of his arms. "Sure as Jehovah is my Witness, like the good Judge says," she shouted, "I'm finally going to get me a answer. How many tablecloths was there, boy — family, company and show?"

Mr. Smart spoke up. "Looked into it myself, ma'am," he said, "and I can assure you it was six, two and zero."

"Praise the Lord! I just knowed that's the way it were. That no-good little girl didn't do a bit better'n I done, spite of all her airs." She hugged me, kissed Uncle Eph, and shook hands with Mr. Smart.

That evening relatives came by to see Mary's boy. I had probably met most of them at the funeral, but I didn't really remember any of them. I had been too stricken and confused to take much note of anything or anyone. I couldn't keep the names and relationships straight. My mother had been the youngest of a very big family, and some of her nieces and nephews were years older than she. I was meeting second and third cousins and first cousins twice removed. Everybody but me seemed to know exactly how everyone was related.

Aunt Muffie planted me on a stool in the middle of the front porch, where they could all get a good look at me and debate whether I took after my mother's family, which meant after the blood relatives assembled there, or my father's. They focused on non-Gower things about me — my light hair, spindly build, and long thin face — that must have come from the other side, from my father's side, dividing me from them. Some thought I had the Gower chin, describing it as stubborn-like, but others thought mine was too pointy for a true Gower chin. Everyone agreed, however, that I had the Gower hands. "Lookit the size of them hams," they said, "and him not a man half-growed."

One cousin brought a photograph in a silver frame of Grandpa and Grandma Gower sitting in a swing on the porch of their unpainted ranch house with their nine sons and my mother, the only daughter who lived past infancy. She was a little girl in the photo, standing at her mother's knee, smiling serenely at the camera. Her brothers, already full-grown, stood in a row behind their parents, arms crossed on their chests, black-bearded faces impassive. Grandpa Gower's beard was bigger and blacker than any of the others. It reached halfway down the bib of his overalls. His legs were spread apart as he sat, crowding Grandma, and he gripped his knees with stubby fingers. His hands were huge but the fingers were short and thick. I looked at his hands and then at mine. My fingers were a bit longer and thinner, but I had the ham-like hands of my grandfather, no question about it.

Aunt Muffie had baked cookies and made lemonade — real lemonade, without hulls, sweet with sugar. The men and near-grown boys soon disappeared out toward the garage and cyclone cellar behind the house. I sat on the front porch with the women and children, eating cookies and drinking lemonade, wishing desperately to be somewhere else. We sat for long periods in silence, slapping mosquitoes.

After a while Aunt Muffie looked over at me. "Lookit him," she said. "He don't look it in all respects, maybe, but he's a Gower, all right, just like his ma, just like all of them, itching to be somewheres else, too good for us ordinary folk."

"No'm," I said. "I'm fine."

"Oh, go on," she said. "Go on out to the garage with the rest of 'em. I'll pray for your everlasting soul but nothing more I can do for you, you being a Gower and all."

So I went out behind the house and made a discovery that perhaps shouldn't have surprised me, but did. Being a Gower — a male Gower, at least — meant being a drinker. My mother had been opposed to alcohol in all its forms, but the Gower men and most of the boys who'd disappeared so quickly from the porch were jammed in the garage with the doors half-closed, sitting on nail kegs and passing bottles back and forth in the dimness. They were laughing and easy, swapping gossip and hoorawing one another.

"Well, lookit who's here," Uncle Ben Gower said. He was my mother's oldest brother, who was already married and a father several times over before she was born. Uncle Eph had told me that Uncle Ben used to be a house builder but was now all stove-up and living on the county, augmenting his income by bootlegging. "Mary's boy. I about concluded you was going to stay up there drinking lemonade with the women."

He offered me his bottle. "No, thank you, Uncle Ben," I said. "My mother wouldn't want me to."

"A wonderful woman, Mary was, I always heard, but Temperance, I suppose," said a drinker who wasn't really a Gower, but married to one. He was a younger man than Uncle Ben, by quite a bit. He was a brakeman on the Fort Worth & Denver and had on his brakeman's cap.

"All the Gower women most generally is Temperance, but Mary weren't always a teetotaler, not in her young days," Uncle Ben said.

He handed me his bottle again. I gagged on the smell just getting it to my lips, but I tipped it up anyway, blocking the neck with my tongue. Enough of the corn whiskey got around my tongue to set me choking.

No one laughed. "Second time's easier," the brakeman said, "but watch out for that third time, that's when the world gets all topsy-turvy."

Mr. Smart was sitting off in one corner. "That's the way it were," he said. I noticed that when a bottle came to him he passed it along without tipping it up.

I crowded my way into the other corner, wedging myself against the splintery boards of the garage wall. It wasn't long before the rest forgot about me and went on talking crops and weather and local politics as pipe smoke and whiskey fumes filled the air.

"I never knowed Mary weren't always Temperance," the brakeman said.

"Oh, Mary was a handful," Uncle Ben said. He laughed and reached for another bottle. "Poor old Pa. She like to been the death of him, that wild little thing, running off with that soldier from Fort Bliss, bringing shame on the family. Time was, wouldn't nobody bet she could get herself straightened out like she done, going back to school and all and finding that sandlapper from over East Texas way to marry her. Can't think of his name all of a sudden. Skinny fella, tall enough but kinda prissy. Schoolteacher."

"Will," somebody said. "Will Parker. Prissy, like you say, but a good provider. This boy's father, Will is."

A bottle came by the corner I was in. As the brakeman said, the second time was easier. I got the swallow down without gagging, though my eyes watered and for a moment I thought everything was going to come right back up, cookies and lemonade and all.

We had always lived away from kin, and there in the garage with the drinking Gowers I felt I understood for the first time what a family is. Around me, sitting on nail kegs or leaning against the wall, drinking cheap whiskey made by one of them, or at least supplied by him, were people who knew all the things about me that I didn't know and maybe wouldn't want to know. Among them they were the Hosteen Tse of the Gower tribe.

And what these men, the Gower drinkers, didn't know, the women on the front porch did. Their collective memories held everything about my past, about people I didn't know who were nevertheless connected with me in important ways. They remembered relatives who had lived and died years ago and events that had occurred long before I was born. The shared fabric of the past would be revealed, or possibly remembered but not revealed, one painful thread at a time as they, the men in the garage and the women on the porch, passed around the liquor or lemonade. I did not particularly like my insight into the nature of families, nor did I relish having my perceptions of the world and my place in it reordered by the emergence of old truths that to me were new. But I knew there was nothing much I could do about it. For better or worse, I was a Gower and this was my family.

In the course of the evening Uncle Eph tried to sell the others an Indian pony or two, but they weren't buying.

"Last time I was on a horse," Uncle Ben said, "was when we all went after Mary and that soldier of hers. Inside of my legs was rubbed damned near raw. Two more hours in the saddle and I'd a been bleeding into my boots. Pa, now, it didn't bother him. He was a hard-ass. He could climb on the back of a horse and stay there for days, never bother him a bit."

Uncle Eph got another bottle out of a box in the back of the garage, near where I was. One of my first cousins, once or twice removed, Jimmy Junior, I think his name was, was sitting on the box. He had to stand up so Uncle Eph could reach in for the bottle.

"I used to hear y'all cut his balls off. That Fort Bliss soldier, I mean," Jimmy Junior Gower said.

Uncle Ben laughed. "I reckon you got it near right," he said, "but not just right." His voice was thick. He'd been tipping up the bottle a lot. "What we done was — well, to go back a little. Mary done disappeared of a sudden and it took awhile to find out where she'd gone and who with. And so then we took out after ’em. They was seven of us still alive then, all but Dunc and Nate, and we all went. Couple of my boys wanted to go along for the sport, but Pa wouldn’t have it. It was up to him and us brothers to handle our sister’s shame and disgrace, he said, and no need for nobody else to mix in, not even kin. So there we went, Pa out in front, whipping up that old mare of his, riding around the clock, first dust and then rain, riding across the prairie toward what used to be Indian Territory, and him not paying no mind to nothing but the thought of his little fifteen-year-old daughter bouncing along ahead of us in a goddam buckboard with a fornicating private soldier from Fort Bliss whose daddy was said to be running sheep up there in the Territory somewheres. Oh, I tell you, that was hard on Pa, him being not just a Texan but a cowman too, and a major in the Confederate Army when he weren’t twenty years old, and here his baby daughter has up and ran off with a good-for-nothing Yankee sheepherder’s son who don’t even have a stripe on his arm.

“We rode and rode. They had a whole day and night’s start on us, and could have got away had that soldier not supposed he’d give us the slip by heading west and then south before turning back north again. So the time comes and we catch ’em. And that little girl, no bigger’n a minute — like all Gower women she was about as tiny as us Gower men is big — that little girl, she stands up to Pa, scared of him though she was. She says, Pa, she says, I love him and I’m aiming to marry him. And Pa says, You just bet you’re going to marry him, you open-kneed little slut, because you maybe got something of his you can’t give back. And we took ’em on into town, forget what town, but couldn't find us a justice of the peace to marry them, Mary and her goddam soldier. And so Pa put her in the buckboard her soldier had drove her off in, put her in the buckboard and tied her down and took her home, with her screaming and raging the whole way. And the rest of us, we — "

"Well," said Uncle Eph, standing up, "that's enough. Time to break this up. Lemonade and cookies back on the porch."

Uncle Ben kept talking but a lot of what he said was lost in the bustle of uncles and cousins by blood and marriage to the second and third remove getting to their feet and taking one last drink. I heard him say, "And when her baby come, it was born dead, buried out there with Ma and Pa like it was theirs, not Mary's, though Ma was near to sixty years old then if she was a day. And now Mary's out there too, all of 'em together." Uncle Ben shook his head and wiped his eyes.

All my uncles were standing now, five of them — Ben and Jim, Amos, John and Eph, all the Gower boys still living. They seemed to fill the garage, tall men, beardless now and gray but still broad-faced, with heavy shoulders and drinkers' bellies. They blocked what little light there was coming through the half-closed doors of the garage, bulky figures silhouetted against the night sky.

"We don't talk about all that," Uncle Eph said, not to his brothers, of course, but to the rest of us. "We don't talk about none of that at all."

We went back to the porch. The lemonade and cookies were gone and people were leaving. Aunt Muffie was standing just inside the screen door, away from the mosquitoes, her hands folded over her chest and her lips moving, not saying a word to anyone present.

10

I got up at first light and slipped out of the house before either Aunt Muffie or Uncle Eph was stirring. I walked under a star-littered sky along the dusty road that passed in front of the second-hand furniture store. It wasn't far to the cemetery, not above a mile. The gates weren't open yet, but I crawled over the fence and found the Gower plot where my mother was buried.

There were only two headstones. The big one was for my grandparents. It was of some chalky white stone that had weathered badly. I could barely make out their names and dates. My grandfather had died years before my grandmother and the stone had been put up then, with everything filled in but the date of her death. That blank had never been filled in. I knew the date, however. My grandmother died the day I was born, and my mother had not been able to go home to the funeral. I wondered if she would have gone had I not come along when I did. I had always supposed she would, but now I was not sure. Had she gone home, wanting to, the date of her mother's death would have been filled in. That much I felt sure of.

The other stone in the plot where my mother was buried was a small slab of polished black marble. Carved on it was nothing but a name: Nellie. I stood for a while at the head of my mother's unmarked grave, about where the stone should have been that Uncle Eph took the money for but did not buy. I tried to remember times when she spoke of the sister — her sister — who had died in infancy, but I could not recall that she ever said much more than that there had been such a child. I wished she had told me the truth about her, had told me it was my sister who had been born and died and was buried here. I wished she had at least told me her name.

Somewhere in the distance I heard a cock crowing. Soon a couple of donkeys started talking back and forth.

I thought about my mother, about her being a wild little thing who'd been willing to take a drink as a girl, a handful who had run off with a soldier and had a baby. And I thought about that baby, buried here at the foot of my grandparents' graves, next to my mother. Her mother too. That baby, about whom I had never heard except as being my mother's youngest sister who had died at birth nearly twenty years before I was born, that baby, I knew now, was my sister, half-sister anyway, and my mother had been her mother too. Was she what my mother used to see at those times when I felt she was looking at me and seeing something or someone else? I did not know what to think about that. Or about any of it. I was viewing my mother in a light I had not dreamed of. The picture of her as a handful and a wild thing that Uncle Ben had drawn — was it true? I did not want to believe him, but what he said had been endorsed, or at least not contradicted, by Uncle Eph and her other brothers, who had known her just as well as Uncle Ben.

A wild thing? I thought about that. To me she had always seemed fully formed, a constant in my life from the earliest moment I could remember and mostly always the same. Looking back I could not remember her ever being anything except what I expected her to be — not always fully predictable, perhaps, but always kind and loving, always reliable, doing what I knew to be the right thing even when what she did was make me stop doing something I wanted to do. I had trouble thinking of her as having had a life without me, before me, which had left her with thoughts and memories — feelings, too — she had not wanted me to know about and had given me no hint of.

I stretched out on the ground between my mother's grave and my sister's and stared at the sky. It was getting bright now and the stars faded away. The sun would pop up any minute. I thought about the photographs I had seen of my mother as a child with her family and as a young girl with my grandfather and Teddy Roosevelt. I wondered why she had not shown those photographs to me — why, in fact she had never shown me a single picture of my grandparents and uncles. In coming after her and tearing her away from the young soldier she had never mentioned to me but must have loved, had they so embittered her that she had not wanted to see them even in a picture, had not wanted me to see them either?

I realized, in thinking back, that what she had told me about growing up were mostly comic tales. All I had learned from her about her family were the jokes, the clownish images — her father in his outlandish farmer's garb picking his teeth with his knife blade at the Sunday dinner table while her hulking brothers debated how many angels could stand on the head of a pin, finally spilling out into the yard to settle the question with their fists. Even the death of Uncle Dunc had seemed more funny than tragic as she told it — the nearsighted marshal banging away at a statue he mistook for a bankrobber while the bankrobber took deadly aim at him. The hanging had been uncomic, of course. She wept as she told me about it, about the horror she felt and about the cruel teacher who had forced her to watch a young man's body jerk at the end of a rope until Uncle Eph came to her aid.

More questions flooded my mind. She would have been sixteen when my sister was born and twenty-five when she met my father, ten years before I came along. How had she filled those intervening years? How had a wild little thing turned herself into the teacher whose first job was in a two-room school of which my father was the principal?

She had told me the story of her first job many times and how she managed to get fired, taking my father with her. She was a strong believer in the rights of women and organized a suffragette march in the little East Texas farm town where she met my father. Wearing sunbonnets to shield their faces from the scorn of the hooting populace, she and three other young women marched down the unpaved main street on a Saturday morning when the town was crowded with farm wagons. They brandished placards bearing inflammatory slogans, while dodging horses and wagon wheels and holding their skirts out of the dust and horse droppings. The farm women they hoped to reach with their message of equal rights turned their faces away as the men spat tobacco juice in the dust. Only my father cheered as my mother and her friends passed by. The school board instantly convened a special meeting, firing her for marching and him for cheering. Neither of them ever got the overdue pay coming to them.

That story was one of my favorites because it presented my parents in the way I liked to think of them — together, doing the right thing regardless of consequences. I remembered riding along at night in the back seat of our old Dodge, watching them in the front seat. My father gripped the wheel with long, slender fingers, driving steadily through darkness into a saucer of light on the road ahead. My mother leaned her head against his shoulder. I could hear her saying something but could not hear her words or what he responded. They both laughed, looking guiltily over their shoulders at me, not wanting to wake me. I knew messages were going back and forth between them, more messages than words, and I did not know what either the words or the messages were. My parents were a mystery but I did not care. They were together and I was there in the back seat riding with them into that circle of light.

The sun was up now, rising fast in the sky. I got to my feet and my shadow stretched long over the graves.

I went back to Uncle Eph's house by way of the town square to look again at the bullet-scarred Confederate soldier in front of the courthouse. I wondered why my grandfather had felt it necessary to promote himself from private to major, and why Uncle Eph wanted to believe in his majority and my mother did not. She had told me Grandpa Gower was just a boy when the war started, and he had run away from home to volunteer. After the battle of Vicksburg my grandmother, who lived somewhere near Jackson, hid him until they could marry and slip off to Texas. Why it was necessary for him to hide and why my grandmother felt she was the one to do it, my mother did not say and I had never learned. They were not questions I had thought to raise with her, though I had always assumed heroic purposes lay behind Grandpa's need for hiding and Grandma's decision to hide him. With my new knowledge of the complexity of family histories and my recently acquired awareness of the pain, anger, and grief that lay beneath the cheerful surface of the stories my mother had told me of her childhood, I could no longer assume that whatever it was my grandfather did at Vicksburg was something I would admire. One more mystery.

I wondered if my father knew about my mother as a wild thing, about Nellie. It was a question I did not know how I could ever ask. It seemed to me that if he knew he would not want me to know, and if he did not know, I could not be the one to tell him, not now, not with Ma dead out there with Nellie. I felt burdened with knowledge that was not to be shared, like a guilty secret. I thought again of my parents together in the front seat of an old Dodge on a reservation road, following a saucer of light into darkness.

11

In Wichita Falls Uncle Eph drove Mr. Smart and me past the houses he had built in his rich days, them in the front seat, me in the back. Neither place looked as grand as I had been led to expect. They were big houses, bigger than any I had ever been in, but not so huge that I couldn't imagine living in them or what they were like inside. Uncle Eph stopped in front of the first of the houses and pounded on the steering wheel as he described the glorious details that the modest frame exterior hid from our eyes. Fourteen-foot ceilings of carved plaster, oak floors of the highest quality, mahogany paneling, a bathroom on every floor, and a kitchen with a gas range instead of a coal stove — these, Uncle Eph protested, were what we could not see as we drove past.

The house had a "Rooms for Rent" sign out front.

"Look at that," Uncle Eph said. "I can't believe it — poor white trash being invited in as paying guests. In my day folks like that would of been bowing and scraping, just going past."

His other house was all boarded up. It was brick, with a porte cochère. Shingles were missing from the roof and the wood trim needed paint. The sign out front, almost obscured by weeds, said "For Sale."

All Uncle Eph could do when we stopped in front of it was shake his head. He was too upset to speak.

"That house," he said after awhile, "it's got a ballroom, two living rooms — call 'em drawing rooms, if you want — and a bathroom for every bedroom. I tell you, it's the latest thing, never mind it being ten years going on fifteen since me and Muffie put it up. Nothing built today can compare with what that house is. Muffie loved it. There's a linen closet on every floor, and two for the dining room."

"How many tablecloths?" I couldn't help asking.

Uncle Eph didn't hear me, or pretended he didn't. Mr. Smart waggled a finger at me warningly.

Uncle Eph drove us next into another, older part of town to show us the bungalow where he and Aunt Muffie had started their married life. He was just getting into the business world then, buying hides for a harness maker. The little house was still occupied and children played on a strip of grass in front. We stopped across the street.

"That upstairs window, that's the room your ma and grandma lived all the time she was waiting for her baby," Uncle Eph said. "She couldn't stay in Owchita, of course, her being pregnant and no husband, so her and Ma come here where nobody knowed her and we took her in, Muffie and me."

I said, "Where was the baby born?"

"Right up there. Same room. Your grandpa come over from Owchita and him and Ma, they delivered that baby themselves, right up there in that same room. They knew what to do, of course, Ma having had so many kids herself and helping with a whole lot more."

"And it was born dead?"

"That's right. Never cried once. Pa, he come down the stairs, hands still bloody, carrying the poor little thing wrapped in a towel. Next day Ma and him went back to Owchita to bury it. Mary couldn't go, of course, not so soon after the birth. Matter of fact, she never did go back, not so far as I ever heard, not even to see Ma before she died."

"Did Grandpa kill her? Nellie, I mean?" I asked.

Without looking around, Uncle Eph reached over the seat and smashed me backhanded across the face. My nose started bleeding and my front teeth felt suddenly loose.

"Don't never let me hear you say nothing like that again," he said.

"Nosir," I said, crying, holding a handkerchief to my nose. "I'm sorry, Uncle Eph."

He put the car in gear and let out the clutch. "It was a breech birth, you see — damned near tore poor little Mary in two. Pa, he had to reach in there and just pull it out."

I felt angry with myself for letting him make me cry, and sickened by what I was learning. But I felt I was getting to know my mother for the first time as a whole person, not just as my mother, and there were more questions I wanted answers to. Fighting to get the tears out of my voice, still holding the handkerchief to my nose, I asked my questions — what had my mother done after the baby's birth and death? Where had she stayed? How had she lived?

"She stayed with us awhile longer till she was well again," Uncle Eph said, "a real sad little girl, but her and Muffie didn't get along too good. Nobody's fault, really. Muffie was just about having our second and the house was getting pretty well filled up, so she thought Mary ought to go home again so we could have her room. Mary said she wasn't going home again ever, and she wouldn't say she repented her sin or the shame she'd brought on the family either. One day when she was out of the house, Muffie just packed her suitcases and put them out on the front porch. Turned out Mary that very day had found herself a job as Mrs. Dr. Morgan's live-in kitchen maid, so she was moving out anyway, which kind of killed the joy of it for Muffie. Went back to school the same time, Mary did, and got her diploma, and then she signed up at the normal school and got her teaching certificate. She was a spunky little thing, your ma was. Too spunky, Muffie always said. 'There's such a thing as too much red pepper,' Muffie used to say. And then she was full of funny ideas that I don't know where they come from. Lost her first teaching job for putting on a suffragette march."

"I know about that," I said. I didn't say so, but I didn't think letting women vote had been a funny idea or anything more than right. I had been exposed to my mother's beliefs about the equality of men and women all my life.

I had one more question. "Who put the stone on the baby's grave?"

"Mary done that herself, long years after — had it done, that is. About the time you was born, or just before. Up to then there hadn't been no marker on it at all. Fact is, none of us knowed what that baby's name was or if it had a name, but when we took your grandma out there to bury her, there was that stone with Nellie carved on it. Nellie was Grandma Wilkes's name, your great-grandma, and Mary and her always got along real well, not like her and Ma. Mary named that poor little baby Nellie for Grandma Wilkes just like she named you David for Grandpa Wilkes and not Amos for Pa."

It pleased me to know that it had been my mother, not Uncle Eph or my grandparents, who put the marker on the baby's grave. And I was glad my name was David, not Amos.

We drove back through town to the highway we'd come in on. There were a lot of rundown tourist courts along the highway. Uncle Eph picked one out for us to stay at, if it had room. He had me go in and sign the register.

"There's people here in Wichita Falls I'd just as soon didn't know I'm in town," he explained.

"What people?" I asked.

Mr. Smart waggled his finger at me again.

Uncle Eph said, "Never you mind. Just sign your name as David Wilkes from Lubbock. Tell 'em I'm your daddy, should they ask, and Mr. Smart here is your uncle. All Wilkes. Nobody here but us Wilkes."

I did what he told me, knowing by now that in this kind of place there wouldn't be any questions, even about why my nose was all puffed up. The man behind the counter handed me a pencil on a string to sign in with. He didn't say a word until I told him I didn't know what the license number of Uncle Eph's station wagon was.

"Then go look," he said. "Can't register you without we got a license number."

Uncle Eph picked out a cabin off to the side, away from any other occupied ones. It was a lot like the cabin we'd had in Amarillo. It had stained mattresses on the beds and a dirty cot for me to sleep on. There was the usual coal stove for cooking and heating, a stand with a washbowl and pitcher on it, a rocking chair with one arm broken off, and nails to hang clothes on — even another "End of the Trail" calendar on the wall, this one put out by a local drugstore. Uncle Eph had picked up sheets at home, so at least we weren't sleeping on bare mattresses anymore. As soon as we got our stuff inside, I went over to the washroom and splashed cold water on my nose until the swelling went down.

We spent most of that day getting ready for the pony sale, putting out more of the Geronimo posters we'd had printed in Amarillo and buying newspaper ads. Uncle Eph said ideally we'd be advertising steadily for about a week before the sale, but money was running a little short and so we had to get some horses off our hands in a hurry. Otherwise there wouldn't be enough cash to ship the herd on to Fort Worth, where he already had ads running in the papers and boys spreading posters around town. Several ponies had died on the train between Amarillo and Wichita Falls — from the heat, Mr. Smart said — and we sold the carcasses to a local rendering plant for walking-around money, as Uncle Eph put it. Any place he reckoned he might be known, he sat in the station wagon, his hat pulled low over his face, while Mr. Smart and I went inside and did the business.

The Wichita Falls parade was to be considerably scaled down from the one in Amarillo. Instead of a real band, Uncle Eph went out to an old folks' home and hired what he called a cowboy trio — two banjos and a fiddle. The players were too tetched in the git-along to walk very far, Uncle Eph said, so they would sit on top of the station wagon and play as they rode. Uncle Eph was going to make himself up as a rodeo clown, so as not to be recognizable, and help out the music by banging a tambourine against the outside of the door with one hand while guiding the car with the other. I was to follow along behind on my pony with a string of horses that were leadable, if not ridable.

Uncle Eph wasn't pleased at having to pinch pennies in Wichita Falls, but he told me to hold my hat till we got to Fort Worth, where we'd have not one but two marching bands and a whole troop of U.S. Cavalry, not to mention Indian chiefs swooping about in full regalia. Uncle Eph said he felt right good about the outlook for Fort Worth.

Late in the afternoon we went back to the tourist court. Parked in front of the cabin next to ours was a Model A roadster with rusted fenders. Clotie was sitting on the running board on the shady side with her sandals off, painting her toenails red. She was wearing her pink movie-star pajamas.

"Well, look who's here," Uncle Eph said. He picked her up and swung her around, planting a big kiss on her mouth. As he put her down he ran his hands over her, up and down and around.

She scrubbed at her mouth with the back of her hand. "Yeah," she said. "Surprise, surprise."

Uncle Eph went inside to say hello to Clotie's mother.

"Your Uncle Eph's sure got feelin' hands," Clotie said. "He knows everything I got on or don't got on."

She sat on the running board again and I sat beside her. "How come you're here?" I asked.

"Ma and him rigged this up in Amarillo. He wants us to travel with you a while."

I thought about it. "You want to do that?"

She shrugged. "It don't matter. He's mean when he's drinking, but he ain't no worse'n some of the other guys she's hooked up with."

I held her bottle of polish for her while she got back to painting toenails. Uncle Eph had left the cabin door open and pretty soon we heard the bedsprings going. Clotie's ma was moaning and Uncle Eph was calling her dirty names. Then they were both yelling at once.

I stood up and started toward the cabin.

Clotie yanked me back by the belt.

"Something's wrong. I'm going in there."

"Oh, sit down," Clotie said. "Ma's just working."

12

The Wards store had a new manager who didn't know Uncle Eph, so that's where he took us to buy Clotie a cowgirl outfit to wear in the parade before the auction. The dress she got had a divided skirt made out of some kind of brown cloth that looked like leather with white spangles on it. With it came a matching vest, boots, and a white hat. Uncle Eph had wanted her to be an Indian maiden, but he wasn't able to find the right kind of dress on short notice, and there wasn't time to have one sewed. We stood by the front door while Uncle Eph finished dickering for credit with the new manager.

Clotie said she was glad she wasn't going to have to be an Indian maiden. With her black hair, olive skin, and brown eyes, people had been taking her for colored all her life and she didn't want to encourage them.

"Indians aren't colored," I said.

"Redskins? That's colored, you ask me," Clotie said.

Uncle Eph came up, the bundle of clothes under his arm, and we went out to the street, where Clotie's mother was waiting in the station wagon. Clotie was proud of how fair her mother was. She had light blue eyes with no life in them and yellow hair that Clotie said she hardly had to touch up at all. Her face was so thin and her skin so white that sitting there in the front seat in the bright sunlight she looked like a skull with a yellow wig on and blue buttons where eyes should have been.

"I got me a real pretty outfit, Ma," Clotie said.

"Did you thank your Uncle Eph?" Her mother had a high thin voice and spoke very fast. She sounded like she was singing or saying her prayers. "Did you give him a kiss?"

Clotie leaned over from the backseat and planted a kiss on the side of Uncle Eph's face. She wiped her mouth as she sat back.

Back at the cabin court Clotie's mother lay down for a nap. Clotie put on her new clothes and Uncle Eph took us to the stockyards, where one of the cowboys Mr. Smart had hired picked out a tame-looking pony for her. It was a pretty white-footed pinto.

Clotie had never been on a horse before, so Uncle Eph decided he couldn't risk having her ride bareback like me.

"Spoil the whole thing if she got shook off," he said.

He talked the man who ran the stockyards into lending him a saddle, the littlest one he had. The cowboy slapped the saddle on the white-footed pinto and reached under for the cinch. The horse arched its back. The saddle slid off. The cowboy picked it up from under the horse's belly and tried again. As soon as the horse felt the saddle it took off at a full gallop, knocking the cowboy aside.

"I'd a swore that critter was broke," the cowboy said, getting up and flapping dust off his pants with his hat.

He and the other stockyard hands went sorting through the horses again, looking for one tame enough to carry Clotie without throwing her or running away or biting and kicking the spectators. The only really tame horse they could find was the ancient bay I'd ridden in Amarillo. It was probably as mean as all the rest, but lacked the strength and energy to express itself.

"You'll both have to ride Davey's horse," Uncle Eph decided. "Ain't ideal, but kind of appealing in some ways — makes a nice picture, big brother taking little sister for a ride, him in the saddle and her behind, or maybe two little sweethearts."

The cowboy put the saddle on and cinched it up. I mounted and he lifted Clotie up. She leaned against me and held on tight. The horse sank to its front knees and was headed on down until the cowboy lifted Clotie off.

"The brute says no thanks, I ain't gonna play," the cowboy said.

"Ain't there some way we can prop him up?" Uncle Eph asked.

"Not and have him move, too," the cowboy said.

"That little girl don't weigh no more'n a feather."

"That ain't what the horse thinks," the cowboy said.

I was still in the saddle, with my feet braced against the stirrups to keep from sliding down the horse's neck.

Clotie laughed at me. "You look like you're posing for one of them calendars, but I don't think that horse is going to make it to the end of the trail," she said.

I got off the horse. It struggled to its feet.

"I don't know what the hell we going to do," Uncle Eph said. "Ain't there a single other ridable pony among all them?"

"Maybe," the cowboy said. "We just ain't found it yet."

Mr. Smart said, "Put the girl on the horse. Let the boy lead her."

"Mr. Smart," Uncle Eph said, "you done it again."

We all went home, had supper, and went to bed like ordinary people, except that Uncle Eph took a couple of bottles of Uncle Ben's moonshine over to the other cabin to share with Clotie's mother. Clotie spread a blanket in the back of the station wagon for her bed.

In the middle of the night I woke up with someone pulling my foot. I gave a yell before I realized it was Clotie.

"Be quiet, Davey, don't make no noise," she whispered. "It's just me."

"I thought you were sleeping in the back of the station wagon."

"I was, but a minute ago I heard a noise and I sat up and there was these guys out there looking over Ma's car with a flashlight and saying, 'Yeah, this is it, all right.' And they was trying to decide what to do, whether rush the cabin right then or what, but one of them said, 'How we know for sure which cabin to rush?' And another guy says, 'Or who's in it?' So they decided to go get the police in on it."

"Is it a stolen car?"

"If it is, Ma didn't steal it. It was give to her by this fellow in Amarillo, a friend of hers."

I got my pants and shoes on and grabbed the flashlight I'd put on the floor beside the cot before I fell asleep. "Let's get Uncle Eph."

"Him? He'll go out the door like greased lightning. Ma says there ain't hardly a man in town of any account Eph don't owe money to. May even be a warrant out on him. Anyway, last time I seen him he was so drunk he didn't know which way was up or sideways. Ma was having a hell of a time with him. We got to do this ourselves."

"Do what?"

We were outside now and I eased the cabin door shut, so as not to disturb Mr. Smart. It was a clear night, with lots of stars.

"You know how to drive?"

"Sure," I said. "I drive all the time at home." That was true. My father had taught me to drive as soon as my legs were long enough to reach the brake pedal, on the theory that living as far from town as we did, I should be able to go for help if anything happened to him.

"We got to get rid of that car."

The key was in it. There was a little slope to the graveled alley between cabins, so I coasted a little way before I put the Model A in gear and let out the clutch. The engine caught right off, the car hardly bucking, and we wheeled out of the tourist court without lights.

Clotie said she didn't want to take the Model A far, just somewhere it wouldn't be found right away, but close enough for us to get back to the cabin ahead of the cops. Next to the wire fence that enclosed the tourist court's land was a rundown service station and repair shop. Some old cars were parked at one side, and I drove the Model A in among them. Clotie said we had to get the license plates off. I found a bunch of tools scattered on the floor of the back seat and took the plates off without much trouble.

"Who's it registered to?"

"I don't know," she said. "That's why I want the plates off it."

"When your ma signed you in at the tourist court, didn't she have to put down the kind of car and the license number?" I realized I was thinking like a person I didn't know.

"Hell!" Clotie said.

We ran back to the tourist court. The manager slept in a cabin just behind the office, which was left open all night with a dim light burning so anyone coming in late and wanting a room could sign in and take a key without waking him. I grabbed the register and we got down behind the counter to look at it.

Clotie's mother had signed in as Mrs. Wilkes from Lubbock, which she'd spelled with one b. For the car she'd just put down Ford. That was all right, because it could just as easily stand for Uncle Eph's Ford V-8 station wagon. But there was the license number of the Model A, big as life.

She'd signed in pencil, just as I had, and the pencil was hanging by its string right beside us, eraser and all. It took about two seconds to rub out what Clotie's ma had written and write in Uncle Eph's license number.

We scooted out of there and got back inside the cabin just as the cars drove up out front. Mr. Smart was stretched out on the bed, sleeping like the dead. Clotie took off her cowgirl outfit and got over by the cot in her slip. I unbuttoned my shirt and undid my belt buckle so it'd look like I had got dressed in a hurry. I had the flashlight in my hand.

"Well, it was here, I'll tell you that. Wasn't it, boys? Right along in here." It was a man's deep voice.

"That's right, right along here," another man said.

"Well, it sure as hell ain't here now, so whoever was in it has done skedaddled," a third man said. "We'll put out an alarm."

"Let's just check these cabins here, find out what's what." That was the deep-voiced man.

Clotie grabbed my hand. "We gotta do something or they'll find Ma with your Uncle Eph and stick her with whoring again. One more time and she's going to be in real trouble."

I opened the door of the cabin and turned my flashlight on the men standing by a bunch of cars in front of the cabin.

"What's going on?" I said, trying to sound sleepy and confused.

The men whirled toward me. Only a couple of them were in police uniforms, but they all seemed to have guns and lights pointed at me.

"Hey!" I said, not having to fake sounding scared. "Don't point them things at me. I ain't done nothing."

"It's only a kid," one of the policemen said. "Put away your guns. He ain't going to hurt you."

"There's another one," somebody yelled.

I looked over my shoulder and saw Clotie poking her head around the door. She had a big simper on her face.

"My kid sister," I said.

"My name's Clothilda, Clothilda Ann Wilkes," she said. "Call me Clotie."

"What's your name, kid?" the policeman asked me.

"Davey. Davey Wilkes. I heard all the talking and come out to see what's going on."

"You know anything about a Model A Ford parked out here tonight?"

"There was one parked over in the next row of cabins awhile ago when I went to the restroom, but when I come out it was gone."

"Notice the license number?"

"Nosir. It was a Texas car, though, I noticed that."

Clotie spoke up. "I seen it too. Davey took me to the ladies' the same time."

The policeman said, "Well, fellas, there you are. Whatever you seen, it was in the next row over and ain't there now."

"I'd a swore — " the deep-voiced man said.

The policeman cut him off and spoke to Clotie and me. "You kids better get back in there before your folks find you out of bed and tan your backsides."

"Yessir," I said.

"Good night, officer," Clotie said.

We closed the door and leaned against it, listening to the cars leave, holding hands over our mouths to keep from laughing out loud. We heard the cars stop up at the office.

They were checking the register, but that didn't worry us. We knew they weren't going to find anything out of the way.

13

After a little, Clotie went back to the cabin next door. She said she figured Uncle Eph and her ma had long since closed up shop for the evening and she'd be able to sleep in her own bed. It seemed like I had hardly dropped onto the cot when I heard women screaming and a man yelling. It was so loud the noise even woke Mr. Smart up. For a fat man he moved fast. He was out of bed with his overalls and shoes on by the time I was just starting to pull on my pants. I followed him as he rushed out the door and into Clotie's ma's cabin.

Uncle Eph was standing in the middle of the room with nothing on but socks and an undershirt. He was all bent over, roaring like a bull, holding himself with one ham-like hand and striking out with the other like he was in the ring with Jack Dempsey. Clotie's mother stood in front of him, naked as a jaybird, trying without a lot of luck to dodge his fist while swinging at him with a broom. Big bruises were coming out all over her.

"Out of my way, you ass-peddling bitch."

"You stay off the child, you hear?" she screamed. "You want something, come to me. Don't you ever, ever, touch her again."

Clotie was naked too. She hunkered down in a corner behind her mother, shoulders hunched forward and hands thrust between her thighs, trying to cover her nakedness. Blood poured from her nose and dripped off her chin onto her knees.

"I just got in my bed in my slip, Ma, trying not to wake you up," she said, crying hard, "and all of sudden he piles on me and rips off my clothes."

"Oh, you bastard. What you done to my little girl?"

Uncle Eph smashed Clotie's ma across the face. "Ain't nobody gonna kick me in the balls like she done and get away with it."

Mr. Smart jumped on his back and pinned his arms. Uncle Eph hit the floor like a bulldogged steer.

"Get sheets to cover up the women," Mr. Smart said, holding Uncle Eph down.

I tore sheets off the bed. With them came some bloodied rags that I recognized as the remnants of Clotie's slip. Clotie and her mother wrapped themselves up and clung together, sobbing.

"Poor baby, oh, poor baby," Clotie's mother said. "I didn't want this for you."

Clotie said, "I locked my feet, Ma, like you said, and that's when he hit me. I done the best I could, Ma."

"I know you did. Oh, I know you did."

"I got him good, Ma. I give him the knee twice, real hard."

Uncle Eph had passed out on the floor and Mr. Smart stood up, leaving him there.

"Less'n you mean to law him you best be out of here by morning," Mr. Smart said.

Clotie's mother agreed. "Soon's we can pack up the car, we're gonna be on our way back to Amarillo."

I told her what we'd done about the Model A. Mr. Smart thought we'd done the right thing in getting rid of it, but Clotie's ma wasn't so sure. She said it was the first car she'd ever had free and clear and she didn't know where in this world or the next she'd get another. Besides, she didn't have money to buy bus fare back to Amarillo, and after the beating Uncle Eph had given her she didn't know when she'd be able to earn it.

"Listen," I said, "I'll get some plates off another car and put them on the Model A, and then you can maybe drive it back to Amarillo."

It was not the kind of thing I'd ever have thought of a week earlier, but now the idea just seemed to pop into my head, like stealing a new set of plates to put on a stolen car was the natural thing to do.

I walked along the rows of cabins until I found an old Plymouth parked a little aside in some shadows and switched its plates with those Clotie and I had taken off the Model A earlier. I took the new plates over to the service station and put them on Clotie's mother's car. It was almost morning by then, but still dark. Making sure no one was around, I cranked the starter and drove back without lights.

Clotie and her mother were dressed and almost packed. Both of them had black eyes, puffed-up noses and split lips. Uncle Eph was sprawled out on the floor, sound asleep. I threw one of the bloody sheets over him. I didn't like looking at him.

When the bags were ready, Mr. Smart and I took them out to the Model A. Without anyone seeing me, I undid my belt and dug out the two ten-dollar bills Pa had hidden there. He'd said I wasn't to let anyone know I had them, not even Uncle Eph, but I was sure he'd approve of what I was doing.

Clotie came out and got in the car. She didn't speak and kept her face turned away. Her mother was already behind the wheel. I reached up and gave her the twenty dollars. I didn't want to give it to Clotie. I was afraid she would misunderstand.

Nobody said anything. Clotie's mother let out the clutch too fast and the Model A went bucking off.

I slept most of the morning. When I woke up Mr. Smart was sitting on the edge of the other bed looking at me.

"Boy," he said, "I ain't one to interfere, but if you got a mind to head for home, that's where you'd ought to head."

He shoved a bus ticket and a couple of dollars for food into my hand.

I started to cry, surprising myself. I hadn't supposed I would ever cry again.

"Now don't do that," Mr. Smart said. "Just remember folks has different ideas and different problems. Your uncle's got problems like you and me got problems, but they ain't the same problems. You understand what I'm tellin' you?"

"Nosir," I said, still crying.

"Just as well," he said. "But remember, that's the way it were."

I took the first bus out. In Amarillo I went to the Western Union office and sent Pa a telegram telling him I was coming home.

He met me at Chambers late at night. On the long ride home in the old Dodge I sat close to him. It was good to be back, but I didn't feel much like talking. He told me everything that had gone on while I was away. Hosteen Tse had died, a trader over at Split Rock had been robbed by three young white men, and Washington had approved construction of a new classroom at Klinchee and the hiring of an additional teacher. When he fell silent we rode along with no sound but the motor and the bumping of the car springs over rough patches.

After a while he said, keeping his eyes on the road, "Did Uncle Eph tell you about Nellie?"

"Yessir," I said.

"What did you think?"

"Not much. I wondered if you knew."

"I knew."

We rode on into a saucer of light.

I asked, "What did you think when you found out?"

"Not much. Not nearly as much as she did. She was young, you see, and made a mistake."

"Did she think it was a mistake?"

"In after years, yes. At the time she was starved for affection and wanted to get away from that whiskey-swilling old father, well into his sixties by then, and her mother, who was so beat down and worn out she didn't care for anything but peace and quiet and no scandal. When a nice-looking young man came around who actually read books, Mary fell in love, or thought she did, which is pretty much the same thing at that age or any age."

"And they killed him?"

"She never knew for sure, or whether they just scared him away from that part of the country. All she knew was, he never reported back to Fort Bliss from his leave."

We rode a long way in silence.

"People grow and change, you know," he said. "She suffered mightily."

"I know."

He took a hand off the wheel and put his arm around me. "I loved her, Davey, and I think she loved me. I know she loved you."

"And Nellie?"

"And Nellie. There was never a day went by she didn't think about that little baby."

"Did Grandpa Gower kill her too? Nellie, I mean."

"Mary always thought so."

"Why didn't Grandma stop him?"

"She was an old lady then, worn out from too many kids and too little consideration."

"She could have tried."

"That's what Mary always thought. That's why she wouldn't go see her mother, even when she went home to put the stone on Nellie's grave, not long before you were born. I reckon, though, that your grandma didn't have the spunk Mary had. Or maybe she used it all up hiding your grandpa after he deserted, when she wasn't any older than you are now."

"Uncle Eph and the others said he was a major, a hero."

"Your great-grandma Wilkes told your mother the real story while Mary was growing up and not getting along very well at home. Later your ma took the trouble to look it up in Confederate Army records, and sure enough, there it was, Private Amos Gower, Deserter. He hid out for most of two years in the woods and river bottoms around your great-grandpa Wilkes's little farm, with your grandma slipping him food to live on. And when the family went to Texas after the surrender, he followed along, with her still feeding him on the sly. About the time Uncle Ben came along, maybe a little before, they were married."

I mulled over all this for awhile, thinking about different kinds of families and different kinds of love, and then I began to tell him about my trip with Uncle Eph. I told him a lot, but not all of it. I didn't mention Clotie or lying to the police or switching license plates. I did tell him, though, about there being no marker on my mother's grave, and how Uncle Eph stole my money.

"I don't much like Uncle Eph anymore," I confessed.

"I never did, much," he said.

"Why did Ma like him?"

"Because he was the only one of that whole crew who ever treated her kindly when she needed help."

With my father's arm around my shoulders, I thought about what I had learned, not just about my mother but about myself. I felt I understood at last what she saw those times she looked at me, her face still, and did not see me. I fell asleep in the front seat of the Dodge and slept the rest of the way to Klinchee.

In the weeks that followed we got an occasional postcard from Uncle Eph. Wichita Falls did not respond to his message of economic salvation through horseflesh. Neither did Fort Worth, despite a full band, the U.S. Cavalry and Boy Scouts whooping and hollering in Indian costumes. Uncle Eph and Mr. Smart took the ponies to San Antonio and Houston, on to Laredo and out to El Paso before Uncle Eph gave up on trying to bring Texas back to greatness. After he and Mr. Smart sold the remaining ponies to Swift for dog food and settled accounts, they walked away with a total loss on the venture of $125 each.

Uncle Eph looked on the bright side as usual. "That is not much to pay for an Education like I got," he wrote. He said he had decided to get back into the wildcatting game and wondered if my father would be interested in staking him. He never mentioned Clotie or her mother. To this day I don't know if they made it to Amarillo or if that was where they were heading.